W9-DEU-870

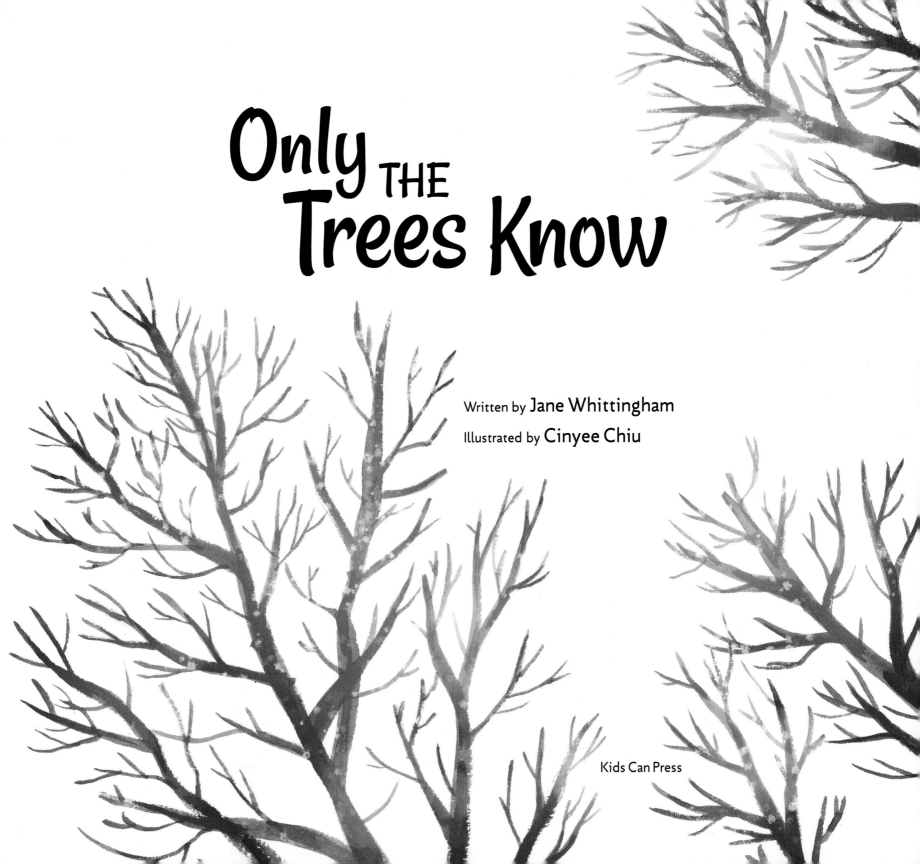

Only THE Trees Know

Written by **Jane Whittingham**

Illustrated by **Cinyee Chiu**

Kids Can Press

Winter in the Old Forest was cold, dark and very long.

The winds blew and bit, the trees shivered and shook, and the snow fell and fell until it seemed that the whole world was covered in a thick white blanket.

Many of Little Rabbit's friends had left the Old Forest for warmer places. Others lay curled up in their burrows, waiting for spring to return.

Little Rabbit was hungry, bored and very tired of winter.

His thick fur coat kept him toasty warm, so he didn't feel winter's chill.

But he missed the sunny days of spring, when he had fresh grass to eat, soft meadows to leap through and plenty of friends to play with.

"When will it be spring?" Little Rabbit asked his parents.

"Winter will move on when it is ready. You have to wait, Little Rabbit," said his mama.

"Spring will come in its own time. Be patient, Little Rabbit," said his papa.

Little Rabbit didn't like waiting, and he didn't like being patient.

He decided to ask Grandmama Rabbit.
She was the oldest, wisest rabbit in the
entire forest. Surely, *she* would know when
spring would come.

"When will it be spring?" Little Rabbit
asked.

"Spring will come, Little Rabbit, but only
the trees know when. Ask them, and they
will tell you," said his grandmama.

So Little Rabbit went to see the trees, which
shivered and shook in the blowing, biting wind.
Little Rabbit looked up, up, up.
He cleared his throat.
"Excuse me," he said. "When will it be spring?"
Little Rabbit waited.
But the trees didn't answer.

Maybe, thought Little Rabbit, the trees
hadn't noticed him. He *was* a little rabbit, and
the trees were very tall.

Little Rabbit balanced on his tippy toes,
and he stood on his head.

He waved his paws, and he wiggled his ears.

He jumped up and down and spun around
until he was dizzy.

Still the trees didn't answer.

Maybe, thought Little Rabbit, the trees hadn't heard him. He did have a little rabbit voice, and the trees stood so high above him.

Little Rabbit shouted up to the spindly branches, and he shouted into the sturdy trunks.

He shouted in a high voice, and he shouted in a low voice.

He shouted and shouted until his throat was sore.

Still the trees didn't answer.

Maybe, thought Little Rabbit, he hadn't heard their answer. He was proud of his ears, but they *were* still little rabbit ears, and the trees were so very big.

Little Rabbit pressed his ears against the knobby bark, and he pushed his ears against the ground.

He pressed them against one tree, and he pushed them against another.

He scrambled up a tree as high as he could and scrambled back down again.

Still the trees didn't answer.

The winds blew and bit, and the trees shivered and shook, and Little Rabbit began to lose hope.

He plopped down on the ground, feeling sorry for himself and tired after all that jumping and shouting and listening. He nestled into the roots of a tree to have a little rest.

As he drifted off to sleep, Little Rabbit's nose
went *twitch, twitch, twitch*. There was a smell
in the air he hadn't smelled for many months.
It was the warm scent of soil spilling out
from between the tree's cold, tangled roots.

Then Little Rabbit's ears went *twitch, twitch, twitch*. There was a sound on the wind he hadn't heard for many months.

It was the merry song of a bird landing on a branch above him.

Little Rabbit looked up. There, among the bare branches, his eyes saw something they hadn't seen for many months: the tiniest of buds, green and fresh and full of promise.

Could it be that the trees had understood him all along?

"When will it be spring?" Little Rabbit
asked the trees once again.
    And this time, without a word, the
trees answered.
    Soon.

For my own Little Rabbit — J.W.
For all those who are excited to welcome a fresh start — C.C.

Text © 2022 Jane Whittingham
Illustrations © 2022 Cinyee Chiu

All rights reserved. No part of this publication may be reproduced, stored in a retrieval system or transmitted, in any form or by any means, without the prior written permission of Kids Can Press Ltd. or, in case of photocopying or other reprographic copying, a license from The Canadian Copyright Licensing Agency (Access Copyright). For an Access Copyright license, visit www.accesscopyright.ca or call toll free to 1-800-893-5777.

Published in Canada and the U.S. by Kids Can Press Ltd.
25 Dockside Drive, Toronto, ON M5A 0B5

Kids Can Press is a Corus Entertainment Inc. company.

www.kidscanpress.com

The artwork in this book was created on paper with gouache and pastel and finished in Photoshop.
The text is set in Picadilly.

Edited by Kathleen Keenan
Designed by Marie Bartholomew

Printed and bound in Malaysia in 3/2022 by Times Offset Malaysia

CM 22 0 9 8 7 6 5 4 3 2 1

Library and Archives Canada Cataloguing in Publication

Title: Only the trees know / written by Jane Whittingham ; illustrated by Cinyee Chiu.
Names: Whittingham, Jane, 1984– author. | Chiu, Cinyee, illustrator.
Identifiers: Canadiana 20210342404 | ISBN 9781525304927 (hardcover)
Classification: LCC PS8645.H5695 O55 2022 | DDC jC813/.6 — dc23

Kids Can Press gratefully acknowledges that the land on which our office is located is the traditional territory of many nations, including the Mississaugas of the Credit, the Anishnabeg, the Chippewa, the Haudenosaunee and the Wendat peoples, and is now home to many diverse First Nations, Inuit and Métis peoples.

We thank the Government of Ontario, through Ontario Creates; the Ontario Arts Council; the Canada Council for the Arts; and the Government of Canada for supporting our publishing activity.